Dear Parent:
Your child's love of reading starts here!

I Can Read Books have introduced children to the joy of reading since 1957. Featuring award-winning authors and illustrators and a fabulous cast of beloved characters, I Can Read Books set the standard for beginning readers. From books your child reads with you to the first books they read alone, there are I Can Read Books for every stage of reading:

SHARED READING
Basic language, word repetition, and whimsical illustrations, ideal for sharing with your emergent reader

BEGINNING READING
Short sentences, familiar words, and simple concepts for children eager to read on their own

READING WITH HELP
Engaging stories, longer sentences, and language play for developing readers

READING ALONE
Complex plots, challenging vocabulary, and high-interest topics for the independent reader

ADVANCED READING
Short paragraphs, chapters, and exciting themes for the perfect bridge to chapter books

Every child learns in a different way and at their own speed. Some read through each level in order. Others go back and forth between levels and read favorite books again and again. You can help your young reader improve and become more confident by encouraging their own interests and abilities.

A lifetime of discovery begins with the magical words, **"I Can Read!"**

RUBY
Paints a Picture

by Susan Hill
pictures by Margie Moore

HarperCollins*Publishers*

Ruby Paints a Picture Text copyright © 2005 by Susan Hill Illustrations copyright © 2005 by Margie Moore All rights reserved. No part of this book may be used or reproduced in any manner whatsoever without written permission except in the case of brief quotations embodied in critical articles and reviews. Printed in the United States of America. For information address HarperCollins Children's Books, a division of HarperCollins Publishers, 1350 Avenue of the Americas, New York, NY 10019. www.harperchildrens.com

Library of Congress Cataloging-in-Publication Data
Hill, Susan.
    Ruby paints a picture / by Susan Hill ; pictures by Margie Moore.— 1st ed.
        p.   cm. — (An I can read book)
    Summary: Ruby the raccoon paints a picture which unexpectedly shows the best features of her various friends.
    ISBN 0-06-008978-4 — ISBN 0-06-008980-6 (lib. bdg.)
    [1. Painting—Fiction. 2. Friendship—Fiction. 3. Raccoons—Fiction. 4. Animals—Fiction.]
I. Moore, Margie, ill. II. Title. III. Series.
PZ7.H5574Ru 2005   2004006232
[E]—dc22

1 2 3 4 5 6 7 8 9 10   ❖   First Edition

For Eliza
—S.H.

For Bridget
—M.M.

Ruby wanted to paint a picture.

"I will paint a picture
of the big tree," said Ruby.

She took out her paper.

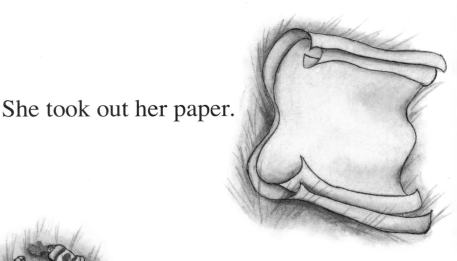

She took out her paint.

She took out her brush.

And she began to paint.

Just then Fiona Fox came by.

"Hello, Ruby," said Fiona.

"What are you doing?"

"I am painting a picture

of the big tree," said Ruby.

"Paint me, paint me!" said Fiona.

So Ruby did.

"There," said Ruby.

"You forgot the very best part of me!"

said Fiona.

"You forgot to paint my red tail!"

"Oh," said Ruby.

Just then Bunny Rabbit came by.

"Hello, Ruby," said Bunny.

"What are you doing?"

"I am painting a picture of the tree and Fiona," said Ruby.

"Paint me, paint me!" said Bunny.

So Ruby did.

"There," said Ruby.

"You forgot the very best part of me!"

said Bunny.

"You forgot to paint my long ears!"

"Oh," said Ruby.

Just then Dan Duck came by.

"Hello, Ruby," said Dan.

"What are you doing?"

"I am painting a picture of the tree,
Fiona, and Bunny," said Ruby.

"Paint me, paint me!" said Dan.

So Ruby did.

"There," said Ruby.

"You forgot the very best part of me!"

said Dan.

"You forgot to paint my webbed feet!"

"Oh," said Ruby.

Just then Carlos Crow came by.

"Hello, Ruby," said Carlos.

"What are you doing?"

22

"I am painting a picture of the tree,
Fiona, Bunny, and Dan," said Ruby.
"Paint me, paint me!" said Carlos.
So Ruby did.

"There," said Ruby.

"You forgot the very best part of me!"
said Carlos.

"You forgot to paint my wide wings!"

"Oh," said Ruby.

Ruby looked at her picture.

She looked at her friends.

"I did not paint your tail,

or your ears,

or your feet,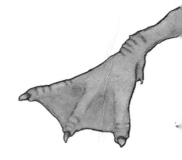

or your wings," she said.

"But I did paint

the very best part of you."

The friends looked at the picture.

They smiled.

"You are right, Ruby," they said.

30

"You did paint the very best part of us."